DELICIOUS!

POEMS CELEBRATING STREET FOOD AROUND THE WORLD

JULIE LARIOS

Illustrated by
JULIE PASCHKIS

BEACH LANE BOOKS

NEW YORK · LONDON · TORONTO
SYDNEY · NEW DELHI

CARTS IN THE PARK
NEW YORK, NEW YORK, USA

Syrian shawarma wrapped in a pita?
Biryani? Pork carnitas?
Maybe I'll get a hot falafel.
Schnitzel? Pretzel? Sesame noodles?
Cajun? Lebanese? Cuban? Thai?
So many choices! What should I try?

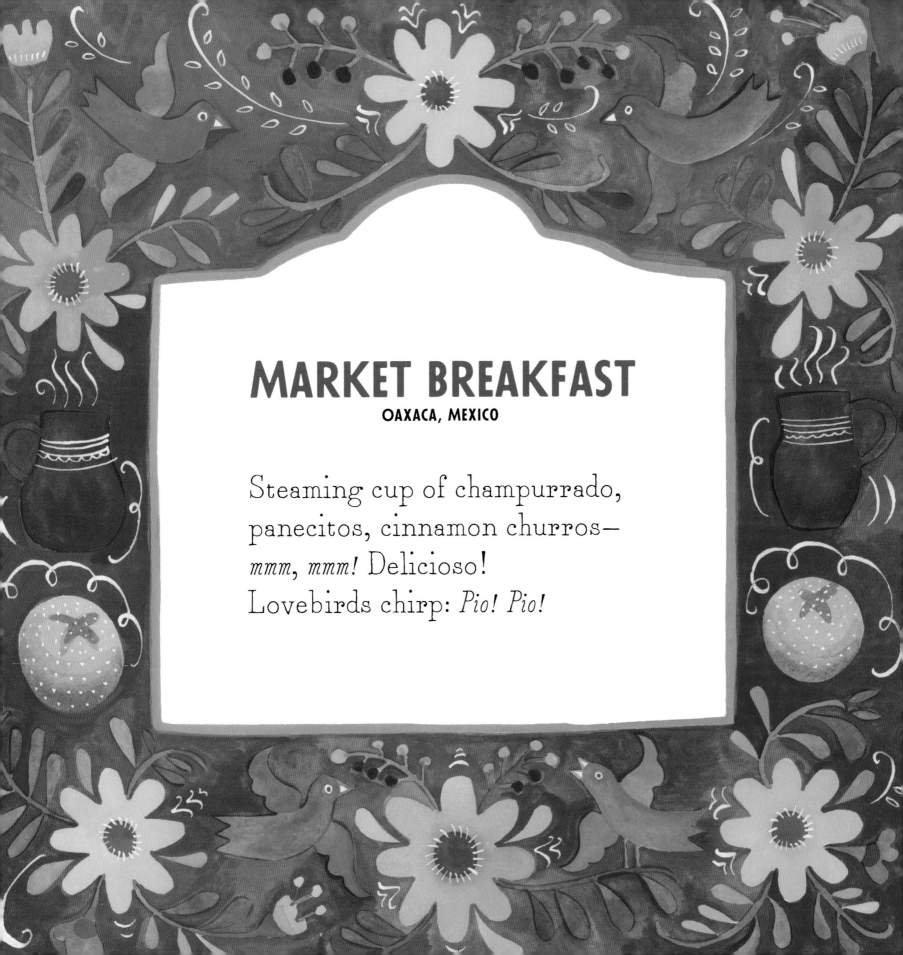

MARKET BREAKFAST

OAXACA, MEXICO

Steaming cup of champurrado,
panecitos, cinnamon churros—
mmm, mmm! Delicioso!
Lovebirds chirp: *Pio! Pio!*

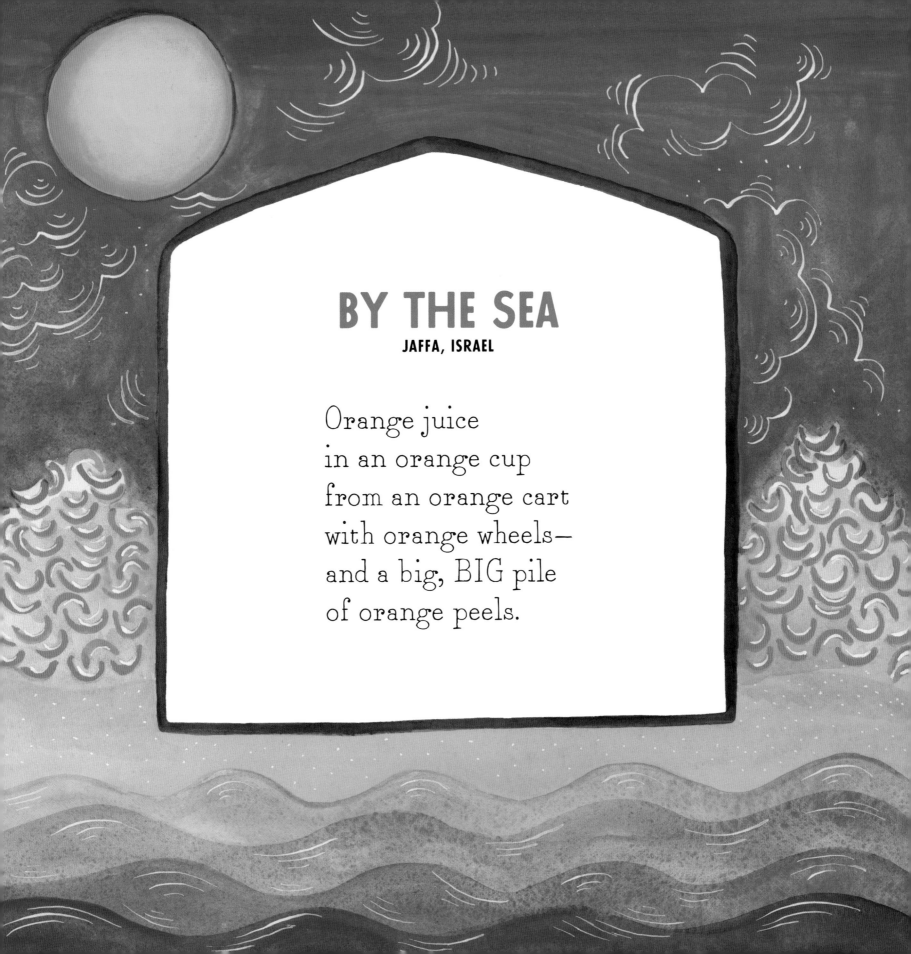

BY THE SEA

JAFFA, ISRAEL

Orange juice
in an orange cup
from an orange cart
with orange wheels—
and a big, BIG pile
of orange peels.

BIKE VENDOR
MARRAKECH, MOROCCO

Old bike with a rusty bell—
tin tags in the metal spokes—
r–r–r–ring! T–t–t–ting!
Mama hears, runs to the gate,
buys us candy, figs, and dates.

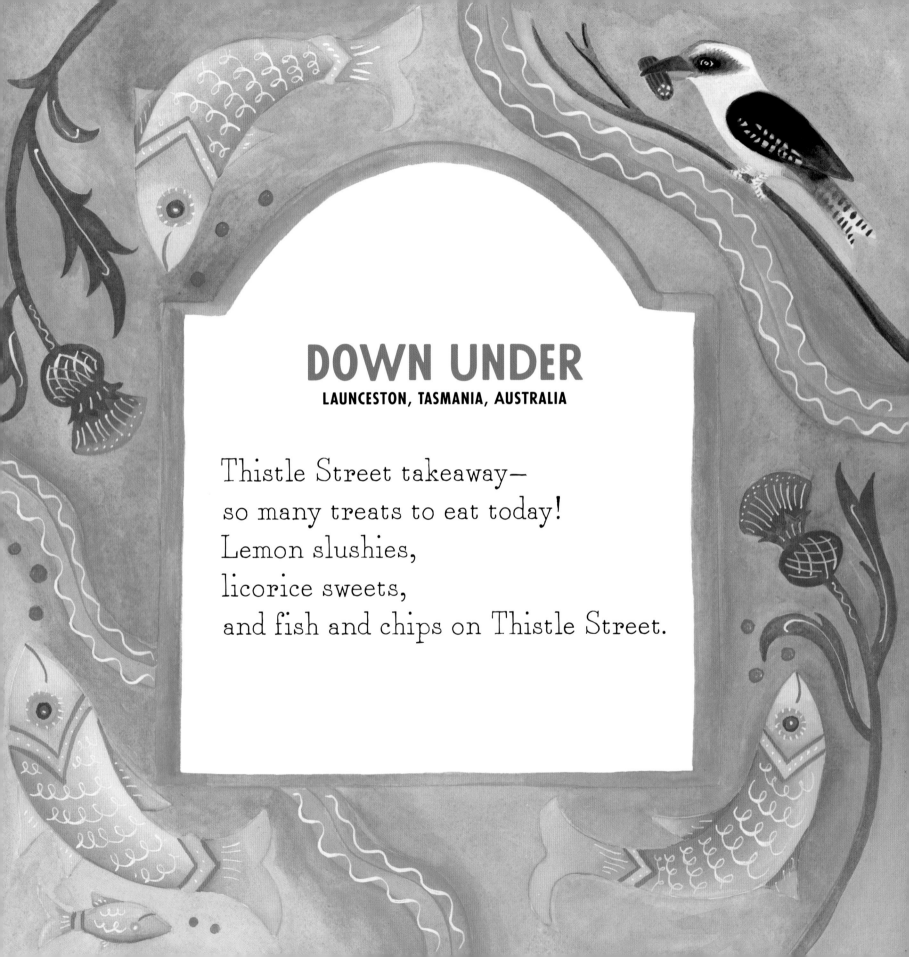

DOWN UNDER
LAUNCESTON, TASMANIA, AUSTRALIA

Thistle Street takeaway—
so many treats to eat today!
Lemon slushies,
licorice sweets,
and fish and chips on Thistle Street.

WINTER MEAL
SAINT PETERSBURG, RUSSIA

Four pelmeni,
three piroshki,
two sweet blini—
one big belly.

STARS

LIMA, PERU

From a tin tray
on parade day
to celebrate the Lord of Miracles—
star cookies, pink sprinkles!

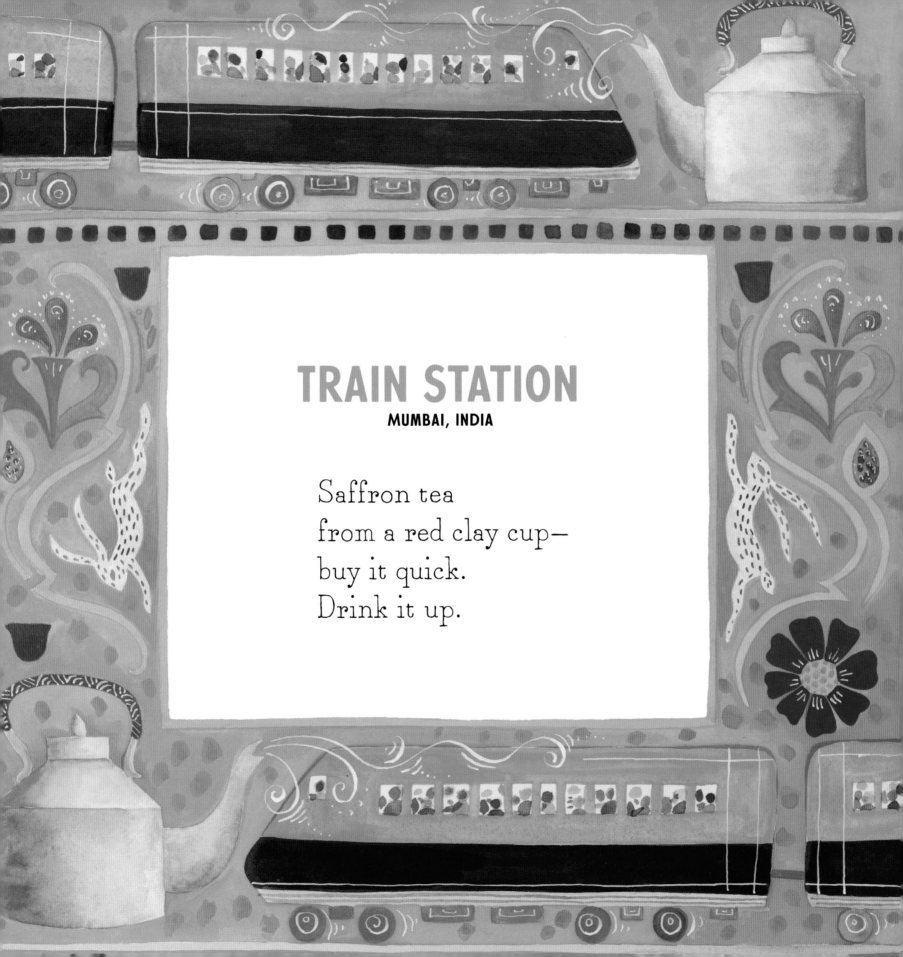

TRAIN STATION
MUMBAI, INDIA

Saffron tea
from a red clay cup—
buy it quick.
Drink it up.

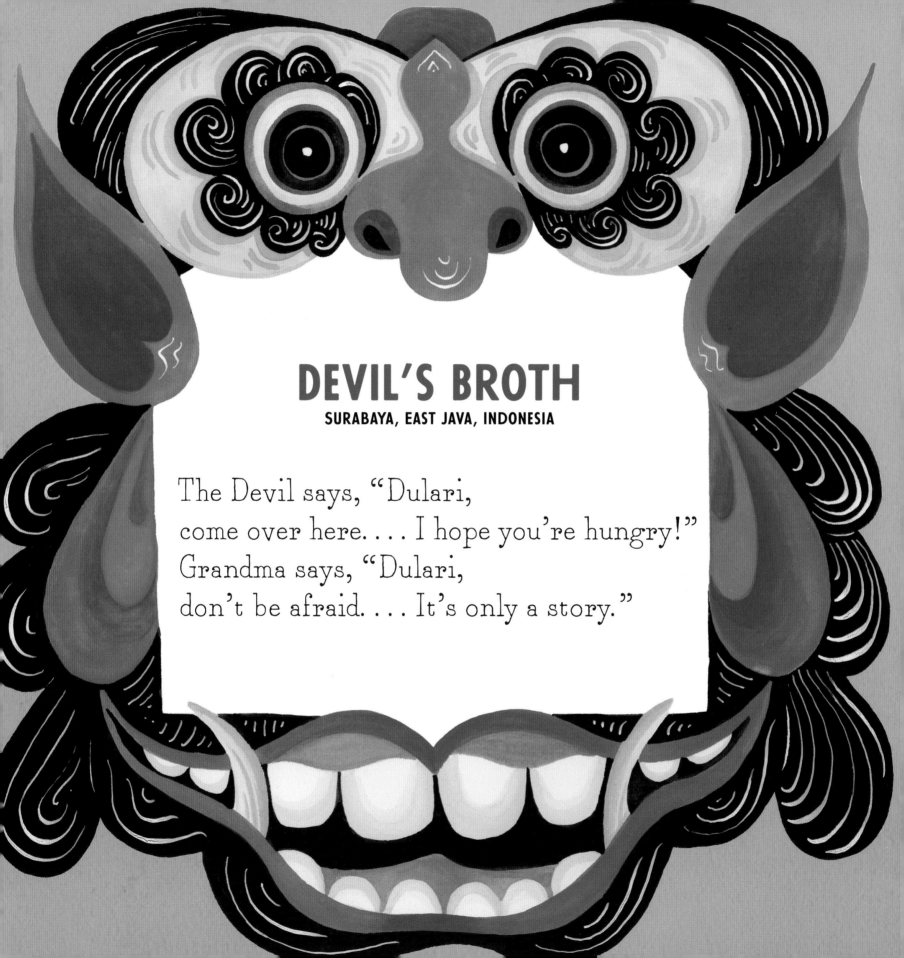

DEVIL'S BROTH
SURABAYA, EAST JAVA, INDONESIA

The Devil says, "Dulari,
come over here. . . . I hope you're hungry!"
Grandma says, "Dulari,
don't be afraid. . . . It's only a story."

BEST FRIENDS
SEOUL, SOUTH KOREA

First full moon day, time to play.
You and I with kites in the sky.
Auntie brings us market meals:
mandu for you,
kimchee for me.

STREET HAWKER
ATHENS, GREECE

Tiropitakia!
Tiropitakia!
Some for you,
some for your ya-ya!
Get them hot! Tiropitakia!

SUMMER DAY
DAKAR, SENEGAL

Cousin, cousin—cold bouye?
Cold bouye from the baobab tree?
And icy bissap water for me.

DANCE CLASS
BEIJING, CHINA

Like little snakes looking for food—
s-s-s-s-s—quiet and quick.
After class, what looks good?
Deep-fried scorpions on a stick!

STADIUM DOG
BOSTON, MASSACHUSETTS, USA

Franks with relish
at Fenway Park,
going, going, gone—
and home before dark.

AN INTERNATIONAL MENU OF SWEETS AND TREATS

CARTS IN THE PARK
NEW YORK, NEW YORK, USA

Waves of immigrants from all over the world have come—and continue to come—to New York City, one of the largest and most diverse cities in the world. When they come, they bring their memories—of family, cultural traditions, and favorite foods—to share. The Statue of Liberty in New York Harbor still stands as America's way to say, "Welcome to your new home!"

MARKET BREAKFAST
OAXACA, MEXICO

Have you ever eaten a deep-fried grasshopper? The markets of Oaxaca in southern Mexico are full of huge baskets of crispy chili-flavored grasshoppers, eaten straight from the hand or wrapped in tortillas. The indigenous Mixtec and Zapotec people play a big role in Oaxacan food, and street vendors sell snacks—memelas, tetelas, tlayudas—as well as champurrado, a hot milk drink made from maize (corn) flour, spices, chocolate, and brown sugar. Mixed in among the food vendors at the markets are stalls selling bread, textiles, baskets, and birds.

BY THE SEA
JAFFA, ISRAEL

The port city of Jaffa has its own variety of orange, known as the Jaffa or Shamouti orange. But sweeter varieties are grown to make the kind of juice sold by street vendors. Other popular street food in Jaffa includes meat with amba (pickled mango) sauce and malabi, a rose-water-topped custard. In Britain, Jaffa cakes are circular cookies made with layers of sponge cake, jam made from Jaffa oranges, and chocolate.

BIKE VENDOR
MARRAKECH, MOROCCO

Vendors on bicycles often go door-to-door in the city of Marrakech, selling flowers, candy, or dried fruit. Others offer services like knife sharpening. In the markets, flower-shaped sesame cookies called chebakia and small cups of a soup called harira are available at food carts, especially during the month of Ramadan, when observers of Islam try to eat only healthy food after fasting from dawn to dusk.

DOWN UNDER
LAUNCESTON, TASMANIA, AUSTRALIA

Tasmania is perhaps best known worldwide for the small but fierce creatures called Tasmanian devils, who live in a broad range of habitats across the island. They are part of the family of animals that includes kangaroos and possums. When they live near urban areas, they're known to have their own version of "street food"—they steal shoes left outside and chew on them!

WINTER MEAL
SAINT PETERSBURG, RUSSIA

Brrrrrr! Winters in Russia can get very cold, so food carts in Saint Petersburg usually sell hot drinks and savory pastries during the winter. But while winter days are short and dark, summer days are long: during the "white nights" of midsummer, the daylight in Saint Petersburg never totally disappears.

STARS
LIMA, PERU

In October 1746, an earthquake nearly destroyed the city of Lima. One of the few objects that survived was a religious painting (created by an unknown African slave), later known as *The Lord of Miracles*. Today, hundreds of thousands of people gather each year to celebrate that miracle. Along with star-shaped cookies, a delicacy called Turrón de Doña Pepa is for sale. Its anise-flavored bars are layered with a honey-like syrup made with cinnamon and cloves; quince, orange, and apple slices; and fig leaves—topped with sprinkles.

TRAIN STATION
MUMBAI, INDIA

Quick cups of hot tea are sold in train stations all over India. As speeding trains slow for arrival, travelers hop down onto the platform to shop; vendors have only a minute or two to sell their goods before the passengers reboard and the trains pull out again. Sometimes, children board the trains quickly to perform acrobatic tricks and ask for spare change or to sell candy from baskets they carry on their shoulders.

DEVIL'S BROTH
SURABAYA, EAST JAVA, INDONESIA

Kluwek (also known as Keluak, which is a poisonous black nut made edible by fermentation) is the secret ingredient that turns this broth a unique black color. One favorite warung (street stall) in Surabaya sells the broth only from midnight until four in the morning, hours that some local people believe belong to the Devil, or to a ghost spirit that walks through the streets of the city, spreading evil.

BEST FRIENDS
SEOUL, SOUTH KOREA

South Korea has a long and lively history of street food. Even the names of the foods are lively, like tteok-bokki (spicy rice cakes) and bungeoppang (red bean waffles). In Seoul, people can shop at the Myeongdong Night Market and eat their street food under the stars. The festival of Daeboreum is celebrated with bonfires on the night of the first full moon of the lunar year.

STREET HAWKER
ATHENS, GREECE

Traditionally, a tiropitakia is a bite-size pie of feta cheese wrapped in buttery phyllo dough. It's the quintessential Greek snack food, sold by Athenian street vendors. Many street peddlers around the world hawk their goods by singing a short song or rhyme about what they're selling. The vendor in this poem is not only naming the snack he's selling, but is telling the girl to buy one for her grandmother, too.

SUMMER DAY
DAKAR, SENEGAL

Bissap water comes from the lovely red flowers of the hibiscus bush. Bouye is a juice made from the seeds and pulp of fruit from baobab trees. Baobabs provide more than just thirst-quenching juice for sale in the markets and streets of Senegal. Their bark has been used to make rope and clothing, their seeds to make oils for cosmetics, and their leaves to treat everything from toothaches to tuberculosis. Throughout Africa, the baobab is called the Tree of Life. Some believe the famous Sunland "Big Baobab" in Senegal was over six thousand years old when it toppled over in 2017.

DANCE CLASS
BEIJING, CHINA

Scorpions on a stick? Really? Yes, really! People who have eaten deep-fried scorpions say they're crunchy and nutty, much like the deep-fried grasshoppers of Oaxaca, Mexico. Along with more common treats like dumplings and noodles, Beijing's Wangfujing Street market is host to many exotic food items like seahorses, starfish, centipedes, lizards—and cockroaches.

STADIUM DOG
BOSTON, MASSACHUSETTS, USA

"Buy me some peanuts and Cracker Jack"—and a hot dog, please! A good baseball game is made even better when you get to eat one of those three treats, that's for sure. In Boston, home of the Red Sox, the stadium hot dogs are called Fenway Franks, and an average of 800,000 of them are sold in a single baseball season.

TO FERNANDO WITH LOVE

—J. L.

TO ALIDA AND CHRISTOPHER

—J. P.

BEACH LANE BOOKS

An imprint of Simon & Schuster Children's Publishing Division

1230 Avenue of the Americas, New York, New York 10020

Text copyright © 2021 by Julie Larios · Illustrations copyright © 2021 by Julie Paschkis ·
BEACH LANE BOOKS is a trademark of Simon & Schuster, Inc. · For information about special
discounts for bulk purchases, please contact Simon & Schuster Special Sales at 1-866-506-1949
or business@simonandschuster.com. · The Simon & Schuster Speakers Bureau can bring authors to
your live event. For more information or to book an event, contact the Simon & Schuster Speakers
Bureau at 1-866-248-3049 or visit our website at www.simonspeakers.com. · The text for this
book was set in 2011 Slimtype. · The illustrations for this book were rendered in watercolors. ·
Manufactured in China · 0121 SCP · First Edition · 10 9 8 7 6 5 4 3 2 1 · Library
of Congress Cataloging-in-Publication Data · Names: Larios, Julie Hofstrand, 1949- author. |
Paschkis, Julie, illustrator. · Title: Delicious! : poems celebrating street food around the world /
Julie Larios ; illustrated by Julie Paschkis. · Description: First edition. | New York : Beach Lane
Books, [2021] | Audience: Ages 4-8 | Audience: Grades 2-3 | Summary: A collection of poems
about street food and food trucks around the world. · Identifiers: LCCN 2020029773 (print) |
LCCN 2020029774 (ebook) | ISBN 9781534453777 (hardcover) | ISBN 9781534453784
(ebook) · Subjects: LCSH: Street food—Juvenile poetry. | Food trucks—Juvenile poetry. |
Children's poetry, American. | CYAC: Street food—Poetry. | Food trucks—Poetry. | American poetry. |
LCGFT: Poetry. · Classification: LCC PS3562.A7233 D45 2020 (print) | LCC PS3562.A7233
(ebook) | DDC 811/.54—dc23 · LC record available at https://lccn.loc.gov/2020029773 ·
LC ebook record available at https://lccn.loc.gov/2020029774